Pickles to Pittsburgh

THE SEQUEL TO
Cloudy With a Chance of Meatballs

Written and Colored by Judi Barrett
Drawn by Ron Barrett

ALADDIN PAPERBACKS
New York   London   Toronto   Sydney   Singapore

Atheneum Books for Young Readers
An imprint of Simon & Schuster Children's Publishing Division
1230 Avenue of the Americas
New York, New York 10020

Book design by Ron Barrett
Line drawings by Ron Barrett
Color applied by Judi Barrett

The text of this book is set in Cheltenham ITC.
The illustrations are rendered in ink and watercolor.

Printed in China
0610 KWO
10 9 8 7 6 5 4 3 2 1
Library of Congress Cataloging-in-Publication Data
Barrett, Judi.
Pickles to Pittsburgh : The Sequel to Cloudy with a Chance of Meatballs /
by Judi Barrett ; illustrated by Ron Barrett.—1st ed.
p. cm.
Summary: Dozing off while contemplating Grandpa's unusual vacation,
Kate dreams about Chewandswallow, where it snows popcorn and rains
sandwiches, and the fate of the falling food intrigues her.
ISBN 0-689-80104-1
[1. Food—Fiction. 2. Weather—Fiction. 3. Grandfathers—Fiction.]
I. Barrett, Ron, ill. II. Title.
PZ7.B2752Pi   1997
[E]—dc20
95-40510

ISBN 978-1-4424-1663-5 (unjacketed edition)

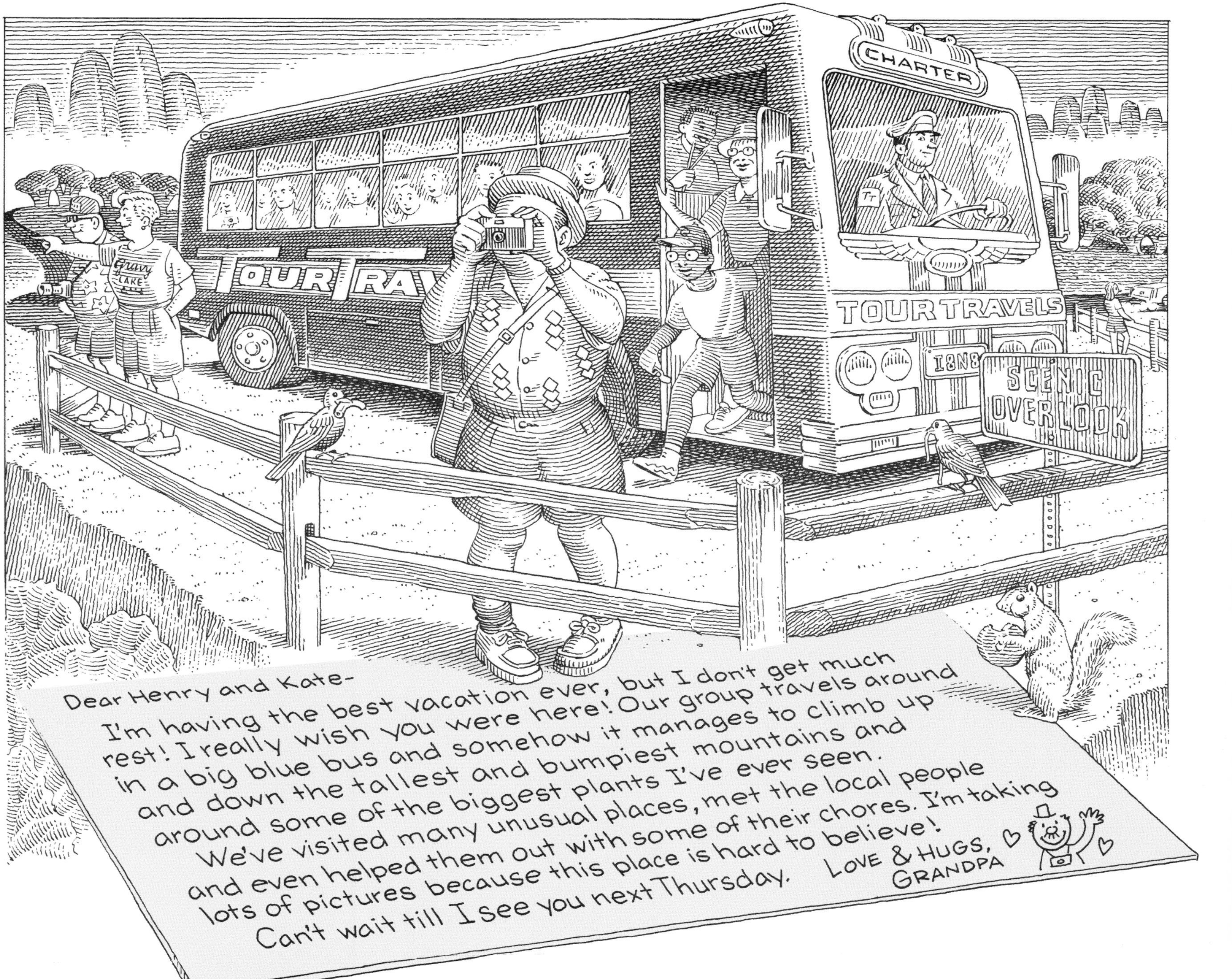
CHARTER
TOUR TRAVELS
SCENIC OVERLOOK
I8N8
Dear Henry and Kate-
I'm having the best vacation ever, but I don't get much rest! I really wish you were here! Our group travels around in a big blue bus and somehow it manages to climb up and down the tallest and bumpiest mountains and around some of the biggest plants I've ever seen.
We've visited many unusual places, met the local people and even helped them out with some of their chores. I'm taking lots of pictures because this place is hard to believe!
Can't wait till I see you next Thursday.
LOVE & HUGS,
GRANDPA

We all missed Grandpa an awful lot . . . his Saturday morning pancakes, his mostly funny jokes, and especially his wonderful bedtime stories. Tomorrow would be Thursday and he'd be home. We could hardly wait to hear where he had been and what he had done.

To pass the time we helped Mom make spaghetti and meatballs for dinner. Henry made the largest meatballs we'd ever seen. They barely fit into the pot! Mom thanked us for helping but asked that the meatballs be MUCH smaller next time.

After we finished eating, Henry and I cleared the table so we could help bake a special "Welcome Home" cake for Grandpa. It was chocolate with strawberry icing and made in the shape of Grandpa's face. We licked as much of the batter off the spoons as we possibly could.

I took Grandpa's postcard up to my room and put it on the little table beside my bed. I kept staring at it and wondering. The lamplight made bright a photograph of a wonderful place that seemed somehow familiar. I said "Good night" to it and drifted off into my dreams . . .

. . . Surrounded by milky blue skies and with Henry as my co-pilot, we carefully steer our plane through large puffs of mist. Soon we find ourselves soaring over an island, a very lumpy island. From the air it looks like a gigantic feast. Immense vegetables, salads, and desserts lie beneath us. The mountains look like huge loaves of bread.

We decide to take a closer look and prepare ourselves for a bumpy landing. Avoiding some broccoli and narrowly missing a tremendous hamburger on an oversized bun, we come down and taxi on what appear to be giant strips of crisp bacon.

Henry and I step down from the plane and look around in awe. Before us lies a strange but wonderful landscape. We are surrounded by larger-than-life vegetables. Nearby is a lake that smells like breakfast, bordered by leafy jungles of lettuce that resemble a tossed salad.

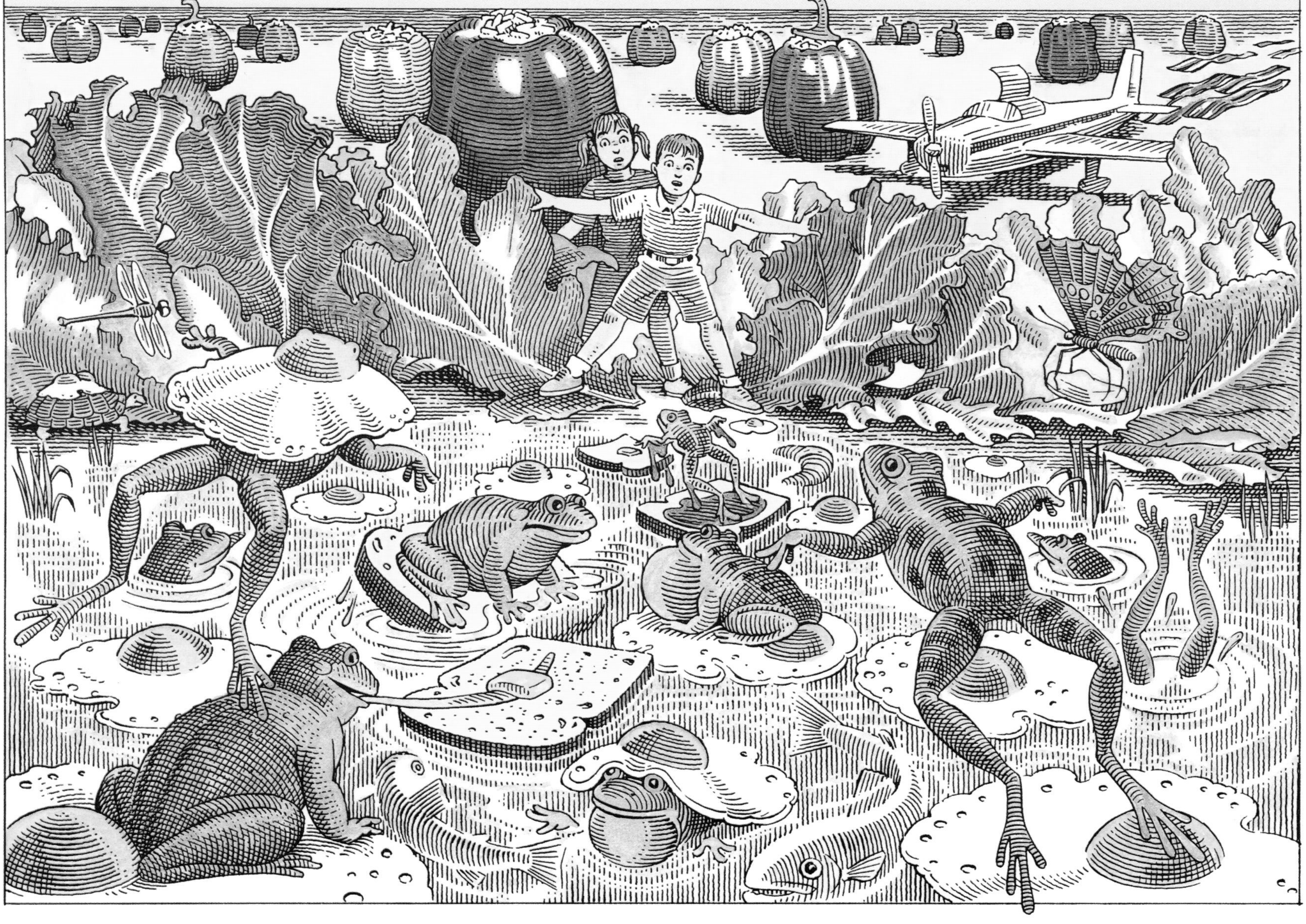

We try to keep our balance as we walk around the top of a gigantic bagel and past a forest of towering carrots. One is pierced by a tunnel large enough for a car to drive through!

Off in the distance we see popcorn snowing down onto the peaks of enormous rolls. Way above our heads, high up in trees that look like broccoli, chubby birds are nesting in huge shredded wheat biscuits.

Ahead of us, at the end of a long road, lies what looks like an abandoned town. Eager to know where we are, we start walking toward it.

Sweet-smelling rain begins to fall. It collects in hundreds of open containers that are lined up in a field beside the road. Lots of orange puddles are everywhere . . . orange juice!

All of a sudden we find ourselves standing in the shadow of a giant tuna fish sandwich being delicately airlifted by helicopter. In the distance another helicopter races off with a jumbo pickle in tow.

When we reach what is left of the town, we see the remnants of a sign welcoming us to a place called Chewandswallow. Somehow, I know I've heard that name somewhere before!

We walk through the entire town in amazement.

Up ahead, lots of workers wearing helmets and dressed in matching uniforms are loading huge potatoes onto a truck.

Other trucks sag under the weight of immense artichokes, enormous eggplants, and massive peas and carrots. Foot-long veal cutlets are stacked up to be packed for shipping.

To the east, the weather is changing and we can see sandwiches raining down. As soon as they land they are piled up neatly, ready for shipment on a freighter anchored down by the shore.

Large reservoirs of milk and cream flow into extra-large containers which are lined up ready to be loaded onto a ship. Printed on the sides of the trucks are the words FALLING FOOD COMPANY—LARGE FOOD FOR LARGE AND SMALL COUNTRIES, FREE.

One of the workers tells us that Chewandswallow used to be a very ordinary little town, except that instead of weather, food rained down from the sky for breakfast, lunch, and dinner.

"Back then," he says, "by some quirk of nature, the falling food grew larger and larger. Storms of gigantic food threatened normal life. So the people took their belongings and sailed away to a new land on rafts made of huge slices of stale bread.

"They returned years later to see what had happened to Chewandswallow. They discovered an endless food supply and decided to create the FALLING FOOD COMPANY."

Now, daily shipments are made to all parts of the world, from the smallest towns to the largest cities. As soon as the food lands it is wrapped, boxed, bottled or packaged, and sent out to people who need it.

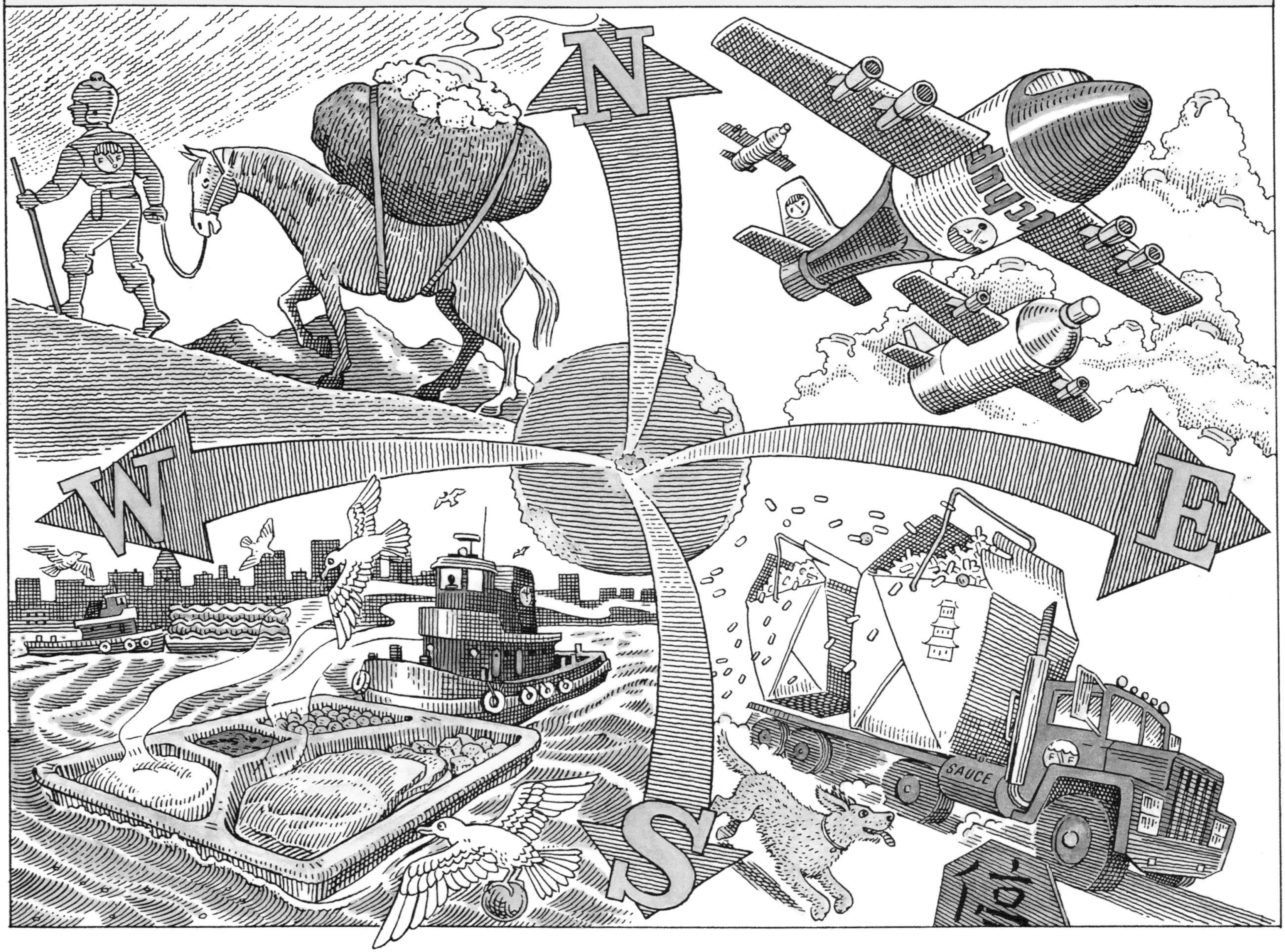
N
W
E
S
SAUCE

Even with poverty and drought . . .

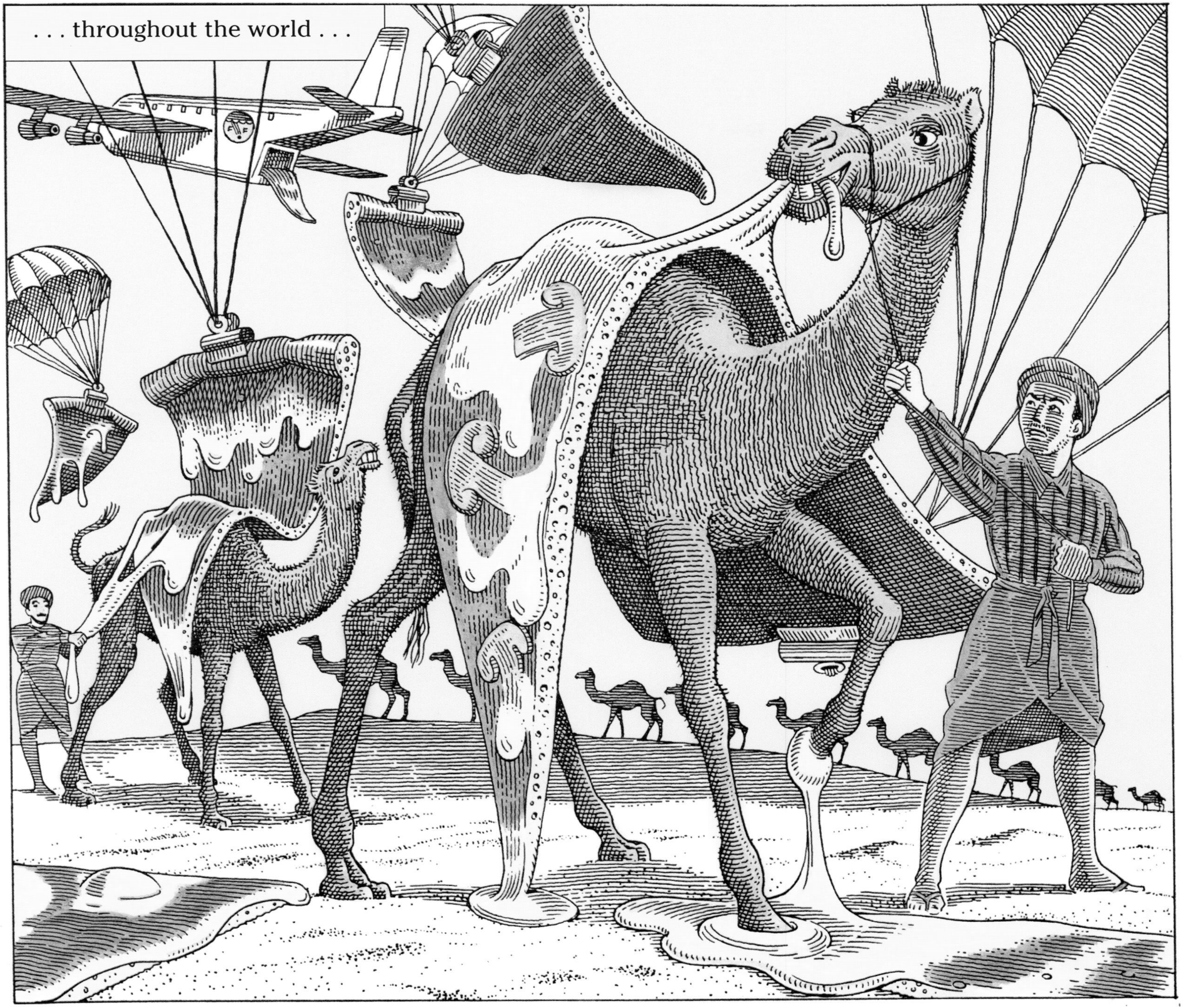
. . . throughout the world . . .

. . . there is always enough food for everyone!

Henry and I think this is a great idea. We wish we could stay and work here but I don't think they hire kids!

It's getting late and we hate to leave but we really have to be heading home. Mom's expecting us for dinner. The workers give us a two-foot-wide chocolate chip cookie which we carry back to the plane. It just barely fits through the door!

We buckle up. I rev the engine and we start rolling down the bacon runway. As everyone waves good-bye we can see dinner approaching from the west. Spaghetti and meatballs I think! As we gain altitude, Chewandswallow slowly vanishes into the distance.

My alarm clock woke me with a jolt. It was finally Thursday and I wanted to get to school fast. The sooner I got there the sooner I'd get home and the sooner I'd see Grandpa!

When we got home, we ran as fast as we could into Grandpa's waiting arms. "I brought back something for you," said Grandpa and he gave each of us a very large box containing a chocolate chip cookie he had gotten on his trip. They were the biggest we had ever seen. Almost two feet wide!

Mom made Grandpa's favorite dinner, chicken and dumplings, and we surprised him with our special "Welcome Home" cake. He chose the slice with the mustache.

By the time dinner was done it was late and Grandpa was tired. When he was all tucked in bed, we knocked on his door to give him an extra good-night kiss.

Then I told Grandpa the most wonderful, tall-tale bedtime story he'd ever heard. It began, "Surrounded by milky blue skies and with Henry as my co-pilot . . ."

Grandpa stayed awake till the very end. Then he looked at us with a very funny glint in his eye and said, "Wait till I show you the pictures I took on my trip!" And then he drifted off into his own wonderful dreams.

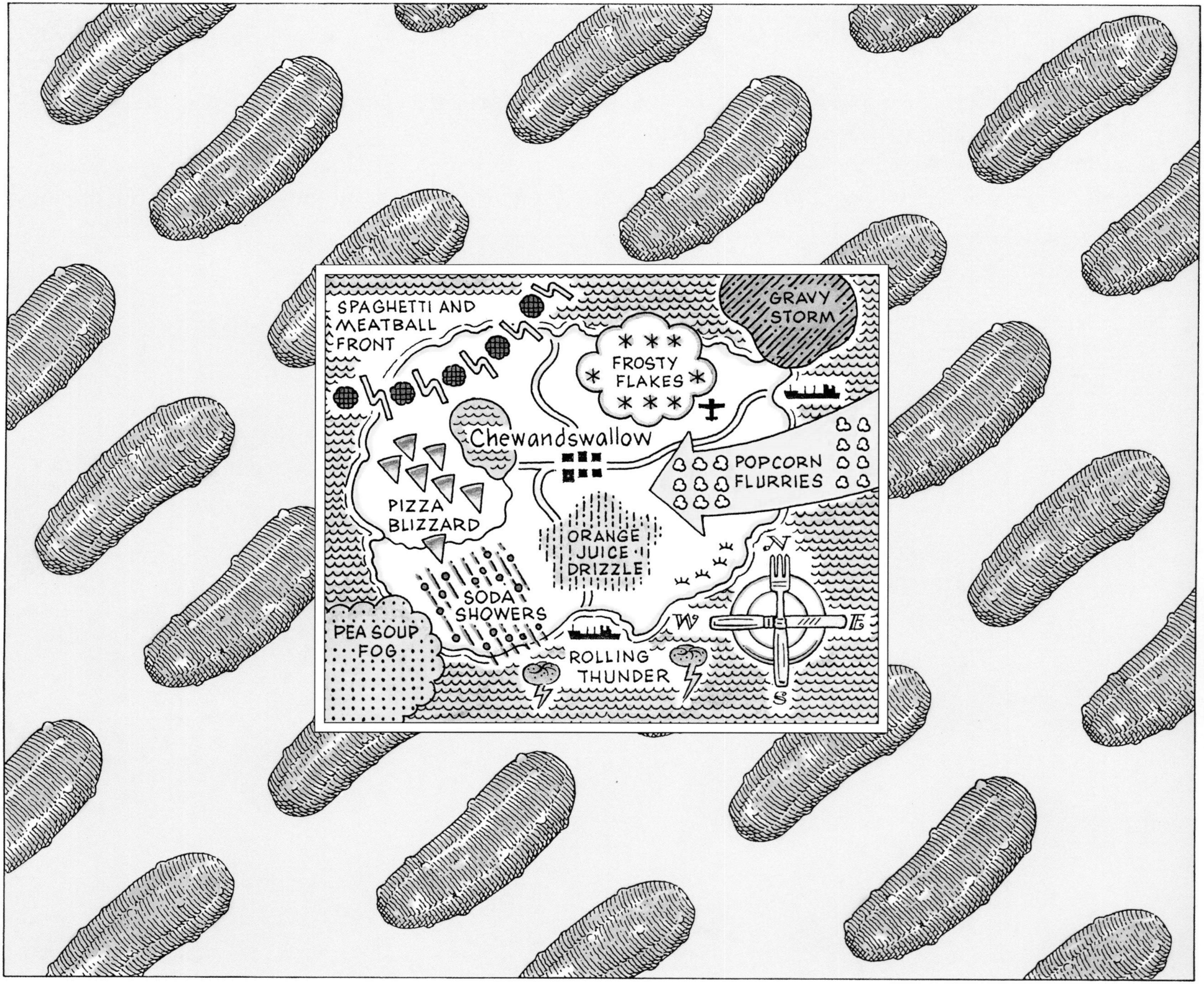

SPAGHETTI AND MEATBALL FRONT
GRAVY STORM
FROSTY FLAKES
Chewandswallow
POPCORN FLURRIES
PIZZA BLIZZARD
ORANGE JUICE DRIZZLE
SODA SHOWERS
PEA SOUP FOG
ROLLING THUNDER
N
W
E
S